MASK

PERIL UNDER PARIS

Welcome to the world of
MASK
MOBILE ARMOURED STRIKE KOMMAND

Imagine a world where there is more to
reality than meets the eye. Where illusion
and deception team up with
man and machine to create a world of
sophisticated vehicles and weaponry,
manned by agents and counter-agents.

Peril Under Paris

The MASK mission: to save the city of Paris
from VENOM's terrible threat – with the
assistance of Scott Trakker and his
courageous robot companion T-Bob.

The second incredible **MASK** adventure.

MATT TRAKKER – SPECTRUM

MATT TRAKKER – ULTRA FLASH

BRAD TURNER – HOCUS POCUS

HONDO MACLEAN – BLASTER

BUDDIE HAWKES–PENETRATOR

DUSTY HAYES – BACKLASH

BRUCE SATO – LIFTER

ALEX SECTOR – JACKRABBIT

CLIFF DAGGER – THE TORCH

SLY RAX – STILETTO

MILES MAYHEM – VIPER

MASK

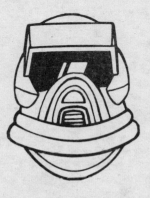

PERIL UNDER PARIS

novelisation by
Kenneth Harper

Illustrated by Bruce Hogarth

KNIGHT BOOKS
Hodder and Stoughton

With special thanks to Bruce Hogarth and David Lewis Management for their great help and excellent work.

Mask TM and the associated trade marks are the property of Kenner Parker Toys Inc. (KPT) 1986

First published by Knight Books 1986

British Library C.I.P.

Harper, Kenneth
    Peril under Paris.—(Mask)
    I. Title   II. Series
    823'.914[J] PZ7

    ISBN 0-340-39891-4

Printed and bound in Great Britain for
Hodder and Stoughton Paperbacks, a
division of Hodder and Stoughton Ltd.,
Mill Road, Dunton Green, Sevenoaks,
Kent (Editorial Office: 47 Bedford Square,
London WC1B 3DP) by
Cox and Wyman Ltd., Reading
Photoset by Rowland Phototypesetting Ltd
Bury St Edmunds, Suffolk

ONE

Paris lay cold and silent in the sombre light. Dawn was just breaking and the sun had not yet risen to warm and brighten the French capital. But even in the half-dark, the city had a stark beauty.

Its buildings and sculptures looked magnificent in silhouette. Its great waterway, the River Seine, meandered lazily along on its way north to the sea. And its most celebrated landmark, the Eiffel Tower, dominated the skyline.

Paris was still asleep but someone was already awake. Lights were on in the Louvre. The splendid palace was now a world-famous museum and millions of people came to visit it from far and wide. It was always very crowded during opening hours.

This morning, only a handful of visitors were there. Matt Trakker, Scott Trakker, T-Bob and Buddie Hawkes. They had come all the way from America and were being given a private tour of the paintings and exhibits. Showing them around was a tall, bespectacled man who wore the uniform of a museum guide. He spoke with a strong French accent.

'It was kind of you to present that picture to the Louvre, Monsieur Trakker,' he said. 'We are very grateful.'

'I'm glad you like it,' replied Matt. 'It's a lovely painting. I thought it deserved to be on display here.'

'You are so generous,' added the Frenchman.

Matt Trakker was a millionaire with his own art collection. What the museum guide did not know, however, was that Matt was also the head of MASK, the unique undercover team of agents and camouflaged fighting machines. MASK was dedicated to the ceaseless task of battling against crime and evil.

Buddie Hawkes was one of its best and most daring agents. He ran the Boulder Hill Gas Station which was really a clever disguise for the organisation's secret headquarters. A likeable and adventurous young man, Buddie had the important job of maintaining all MASK vehicles so that they would be ready at a moment's notice for combat duty.

Scott Trakker was Matt's adopted son. A bright, lively and inquisitive boy, he had a knack of getting into mischief without even trying. His closest friend

was Thingamebob, the short and rather comical robot who was called T-Bob for short.

Matt Trakker was fascinated by the Louvre and Buddie Hawkes was showing a lot of interest as well. They were thankful to have the chance to look around before the crowds arrived. Scott, however, soon became bored. As they entered yet another long gallery, he gave a yawn.

'I don't see why we had to get up at the crack of dawn just to look at a bunch of crummy paintings,' he complained.

'Yeah,' agreed T-Bob. 'Before your dad gave them that picture, we could see it any time we wanted to back home.'

'I've had enough of paintings,' announced Scott.

'This is an archaeological department,' explained the guide.

'A what?' asked the boy.

'There are no paintings here,' continued the Frenchman. 'This is our collection of Greek and Roman antiquities.'

Scott looked around without enthusiasm.

'They're all so *old!*' he protested.

'Very funny,' said the guide, pretending to smile.

'Look at her!' urged T-Bob.

He was pointing at the marble statue of the Venus de Milo, the famous relic which has no arms. Scott grinned and nudged the robot.

'See, T-Bob?' he joked. 'That's what happens when you bite your fingernails.'

'I don't have any fingernails to bite.'

'Neither does she – *now*.'

T-Bob stared at the headless statue of a Greek god.

'They all seem to have bits missing.'

'Yeah,' said Scott. 'And somebody's pinched their clothes. They must be freezing in here.'

'You like our antiquities?' asked the guide.

'Oh, sure,' answered the boy. 'But I wanna see the Eiffel Tower.'

'That's just a tourist gimmick,' argued Matt. 'I brought you here for a taste of real culture, Scott.'

'Well I think I've tasted enough.'

'Me, too, sir,' added T-Bob.

'Wait till you see the next gallery,' promised the guide. 'It contains our most valuable French paintings. You will love them.'

'Don't bank on it,' warned Scott.

The guide let them out of the room and up a stone staircase. Their footsteps echoed through the deserted building and Scott could not resist calling out to see if his voice came back.

They walked into another gallery and the guide indicated the walls with a sweeping gesture of his hand. He spoke with real pride.

'What do you think of these superb paintings?'

'Where are they?' wondered Matt.

'Is this some kinda hoax?' said Buddie.

The guide looked at the walls more closely.

'*Mon Dieu!*' he exclaimed.

'What does that mean?' whispered T-Bob.

'That he's as surprised as we are,' translated Scott.

The paintings were all there but they had been turned around to face inwards so that only their backs were visible. The guide could not understand it. They had been hanging there properly when he had checked earlier on.

'O-o-o-o-h!'

The groan drew their attention to the uniformed figure who was lying on the floor at the far end of the gallery. He was a museum security officer and he was just regaining consciousness.

They raced over and helped him to sit up. Matt Trakker applied some first aid to the wound on the back of the man's head. Slowly, the security officer began to recover. When the guide asked him a question in French, his colleague gave a shrug before he answered.

Buddie Hawkes looked baffled and turned to Matt.

'I can't make head nor tail of this lingo.'

'The guide asked him what happened,' explained Matt. 'All the man can remember is being hit hard from behind.'

'Hey, this is real drama!' said Scott, excitedly.

'Even better than the Eiffel Tower,' noted T-Bob.

'It is incredible!' wailed the guide. 'The Louvre has been broken into. They have got at our most precious paintings.'

He ran to the wall and turned a frame over, fully expecting to see the canvas cut out and removed. But the painting was still there. It was the same story with the others. Everything was intact.

The guide scratched his head in amazement.

'Nothing has been stolen.'

'Yes, it has,' recalled T-Bob. 'There was a lady back there with no arms and a Greek god with no head. Maybe the thieves took *those*.'

'No,' replied the guide. 'Our antiquities are only fragments.'

'It doesn't make sense,' said Buddie. 'Breaking into a place like this and then not taking anything. What's the point?'

'Who would have gone to all that trouble?' asked the guide.

Matt Trakker considered the problem for a moment.

'I think the important question is – why?' he decided.

Buddie checked the windows then strolled over to the door.

'What I can't figure out is how they got in.'

'You think they're still here, Buddie?' gulped T-Bob in alarm.

'Could be.'

'Gee! I hope so!' said Scott, eager for some action.

'Well, you're not staying around to find out,' announced Matt.

'Aw, Dad!'

'You and T-Bob can go and see the Eiffel Tower.'

'But *this* is where it's all happening,' protested the boy.

'I vote for the Eiffel Tower,' agreed T-Bob, trembling.

Matt took Buddie aside so that nobody else could hear them.

'Buddie.'

'Yeah?'

'Take them out of here, will you?'

'Sure, Matt.'

'Something fishy is going on. I can smell it.'

'So can I.'

'If there's trouble, I don't want Scott mixed up in it.'

'You'll have a heck of a job keeping him out of it.'

'I know, Buddie.'

'The only way I can guarantee that he and T-Bob won't be a nuisance is to put 'em in a cage!' He grinned broadly. 'I'll do my best.'

'Thanks, Buddie.'

'Just one thing, though,' added the MASK agent.

'What's that?'

'I'd sure hate to miss out on all the action myself.'

'You won't,' promised Matt.

Scott and T-Bob were searching for clues when Buddie came up.

'Okay, guys,' he declared. 'Next stop, the Eiffel Tower.'

'Hurrah!' cheered T-Bob.

'Can't we stay here?' pleaded Scott.

'No,' said Buddie firmly. 'We got our orders.'

'Gimme a break, Dad,' called the boy.

But Matt shook his head. Scott knew that it was

useless to argue. When Matt gave an order, he expected it to be obeyed. Buddie waved goodbye then took Scott and T-Bob out through the main exit.

The museum guide was still shocked by the break-in.

'What are we going to do?' he asked.

'If you don't mind,' replied Matt, 'I think I'll take a look around on my own. You see to your colleague.'

'But what if you get lost, Monsieur Trakker?'

'I'm pretty good at picking up a trail. I'll manage.'

The guide nodded a farewell then went back to the security officer who was now propped up against a wall. They began to converse rapidly in French.

Matt Trakker headed for a half-open door in one wall. It gave him access to a steep staircase that took him right down into the depths of the building. The further he went, the darker it seemed to get.

When he finally reached the bottom of the staircase, he found himself in a kind of basement. A single bulb threw a poor light over crated paintings and piles of statues. Evidently, Matt was in the part of the Louvre that was used for storage. Some of the items had been there for a long time and were covered in cobwebs. The place was creepy and claustrophobic. Dark shadows lay everywhere and there was an unpleasant smell of dampness and decay. But Matt was quite unafraid. He searched on with the utmost care.

He came to the Louvre that morning as a wealthy American donating a painting as an act of philan-

thropy. Now that a crime had been committed, he became the head of MASK. He knew that he had stumbled on something that posed a great danger.

Instinct took him on, past more crates and more statues that were shrouded in dustsheets. The atmosphere became creepier. The dark shadows deepened. The unpleasant smell got worse.

Matt stopped only just in time or he would have fallen into it. He had found what he was after.

In the middle of the stone floor was a huge square hole.

TWO

The house stood near a quiet street in Paris. It was a large, imposing brick building with two storeys and an attic. Though it was slightly run-down now, the place had obviously been a dwelling of character and had the look of an embassy about it. Set in the privacy of its own grounds, it was protected by a high perimeter wall. Beyond that wall were rows and rows of smaller houses and a few shops.

A long, curving drive ran up to the main door. The entrance to the grounds was guarded by a miniature gatehouse of black stone. There was a heavy portcullis instead of gates and its spikes were glinting in the morning sunshine. The portcullis was in the raised

17

position, its iron teeth ready to drop and bite on command.

The whole place had a faded grandeur to it and a casual observer would have spared it a glance of admiration. But there was nothing admirable about the house at the moment. Far from it. It was being used as the VENOM hideout.

'Hurry up, Dagger!' snarled Mayhem.

'I'm doing my best,' said Cliff Dagger.

'Well, it's not good enough.'

Miles Mayhem was the sinister power behind the villainous organisation that bore his name – VICIOUS EVIL NETWORK OF MAYHEM: VENOM. Arch-enemy of MASK.

Mayhem himself was a big, fleshy man in military uniform. He had wild eyes, a thick moustache and the unmistakable habit of authority. Cliff Dagger was one of his henchmen, a dangerous thug whose ugly face was partly obscured by a cap pulled down low over his forehead. Dagger was used to being bellowed at by his boss.

'Don't just stand there, you idiot!'

'It's not easy,' complained Dagger.

'Use your brain, man!'

They were in a room on the first floor of the house. It was barely furnished and its wallpaper was peeling away. An overhead light dangled from a long chain. The curtains were moth-eaten. There was a table with a couple of cameras lying on it. Pinned to the wall behind the table was a grid-pattern of squares of curling photographic paper. They had been arranged side by side but there were still some gaps to be filled.

Mayhem and Dagger were examining some more squares of photographic paper to see where they would fit on the grid. Each square of paper bore a street plan on it, which was in turn marked with a large cross and some dotted lines. Together, all the squares made up a map of Paris.

Miles Mayhem turned his square of paper around and experimented with it in different unfilled gaps on the grid. Finally, he managed to get it right and let out a shout of triumph.

'There!'

'Where?' asked Dagger.

'That's the Seine there,' insisted Mayhem, jabbing a finger at the grid, 'so that must be the end of the Boulevard St Michel.'

He pinned his square into place on the wall.

Cliff Dagger continued to be mystified by his own square.

'Uh . . .'

'Dagger, what *are* you doing?' demanded Mayhem.

'This one won't fit any place I can find.'

'That's because you've got it upside down, you cretin!'

'Have I? Oh, sorry.'

Mayhem snatched the square impatiently from his hands.

'Give it here! Even you should be able to see that

it only has to be turned up the right way and it will go . . .'

His voice died away as he placed the square in position on the grid and realised that it did not fit. Mayhem now had it upside down. His profound irritation was not helped by the sarcastic remark that now floated into his ears.

'Jigsaw puzzle got you stumped, Mayhem?'

Vanessa Warfield was a sharp-featured young woman with a black streak in her hair. She was wearing a white laboratory coat over her dress as she came out of the darkroom carrying a strip of developed film. Vanessa would have been attractive if it had not been for the malevolent and almost witch-like quality about her.

Sly Rax came after her, holding the last two squares of photographic paper in his hands. Still dripping with developing fluid, the squares started to curl at the edges.

Like Dagger and Vanessa, the burly Rax was another member of the VENOM team. Cunning and unscrupulous, Rax was a dangerous foe at any time and even Mayhem sometimes had a fight to control his minion. Sly Rax's black hair and moustache matched the colour of his soul. He had on his usual pair of sunglasses.

'Here are the other squares,' he announced.

'Let me have them!' ordered Mayhem.

He grabbed them from Rax and took them across to the grid. As he tried to match them up, Mayhem became even more annoyed until he eventually fitted the pieces correctly into place.

Sly Rax watched it all from a sitting position on the table.

'I still don't see why we couldn't have done it *my* way.'

'Who's the boss around here?' Mayhem reminded him.

'You're the boss, boss,' conceded Rax.

'Then don't you forget it!'

'I still don't see,' persisted the other, 'why we couldn't have taken some of those paintings last night while we were inside the Louvre. I mean, we could get millions for some of them!'

'What we could get is caught,' sneered Mayhem.

'Caught?'

'Yes. If the police started searching Paris for art thieves.'

'Mayhem is right,' agreed Vanessa. 'Because nothing was stolen, the police have no reason to be hunting for us.'

'I'm *always* right,' asserted Mayhem.

He pinned the last square in place and stood back to admire his handiwork. Dagger, Rax and Vanessa stood beside him and looked up at the completed map of Paris. The crosses on it formed a definite pattern and they were linked by the dotted lines.

Mayhem tapped the map with his fingers.

'With what we're going to make off this, we could *buy* the Louvre and everything in it ten times over.'

'Why should we buy some lousy paintings?' asked Dagger.

Vanessa Warfield gave him a withering look of scorn.

Miles Mayhem pointed to the map with evil delight.

'That's it!' he yelled. 'That's where the triggering device is hidden. Right *there!*'

'Your finger's in the way,' said Vanessa drily.

'Dagger!' bawled his leader.

'Yeah?'

'I want you to get that triggering device and get it fast!'

'Right!'

'It'll only be a matter of time before someone catches on.'

'I'm not sure *I've* caught on yet,' admitted Dagger.

'That's nothing new,' sighed Vanessa.

'Speed is vital,' insisted Mayhem.

'Why?' asked Dagger.

'Never mind!' roared his master. 'Move it!'

Cliff Dagger ran out of the room as fast as he could. Another deadly plan had been set in motion.

Buddie Hawkes drove along a wide boulevard in Hurricane. From the outside, the vehicle looked like an old Chevrolet but it was full of sophisticated equipment and weaponry. The car handled beautifully.

'Boy, it sure is nice to drive this thing,' said Buddie.

'Then drive it to the Eiffel Tower,' suggested Scott.

'I will,' agreed Buddie, 'if you'll tell me the way.'

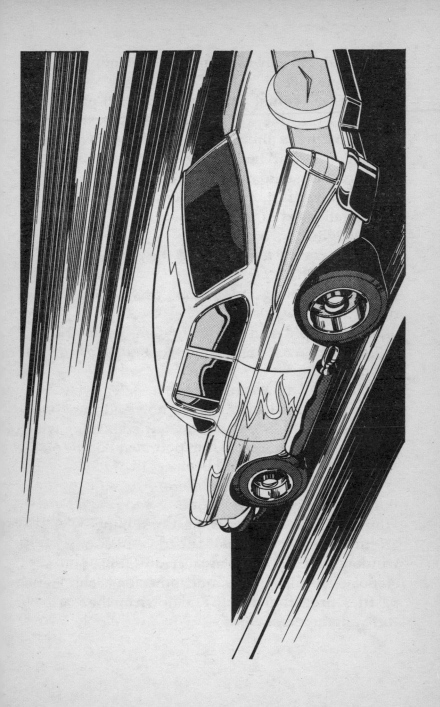

'Tell him the way, T-Bob,' said the boy.

'Give me time.'

T-Bob was getting into a state of mild panic as he tried to work out where they were by studying a folding map. His directions so far had been worse than useless. They had been driving around in circles and getting no closer to the Eiffel Tower.

'Which way is it, T-Bob?' asked Buddie.

'Take the next turn on the right.'

'The right?'

'Maybe it's the left,' decided the robot.

'The *left*?'

'Make up your mind, T-Bob,' urged Scott. 'Left or right?'

'Maybe you'd better go straight on,' decided T-Bob.

'You sure you know how to *read* a map?' said Buddie.

'Of course,' answered the robot, defensively.

The boulevard had narrowed now and a few shops appeared ahead. Scott Trakker saw something which made him very animated. He pounded Buddie on the shoulder.

'Stop there, please! Stop there!'

'Is it the Eiffel Tower?'

'No, Buddie. But it's the next best thing.'

Hurricane came to a halt outside a cake shop whose window was full of eclairs, cream-puffs, jam tarts, Napoleons, millefeuilles and other delicious French pastries. Scott bounced up and down on the seat as if it were a trampoline.

'It ain't like you didn't have breakfast,' noted Buddie.

'That was half an hour ago,' said Scott.

'I feel thirsty,' decided T-Bob. 'Think they serve oil?'

The three of them got out of the car and went into the shop. What they did not realise at the time, was that Hurricane was parked almost opposite the miniature gateway that guarded the entrance to the VENOM hideout.

Inside the cake shop, Scott Trakker was going to satisfy his appetite for cream. Inside the house opposite, Miles Mayhem was trying to satisfy his hunger for wickedness.

The proprietress of the shop was a big, fat, motherly woman with a warm smile. She waited while Scott examined all the cakes in the window and in the glass case that stood on the counter. At length the boy chose a chocolate eclair. Buddie Hawkes paid for it then crossed to join Scott and T-Bob at a small table.

The robot had unfurled his map completely now and was desperate to locate the Eiffel Tower on it. Buddie offered to help with the navigation and reached out for the map.

'Let me have a look at that, T-Bob,' he suggested. 'I get the feeling we're nowhere near the Eiffel Tower.'

The robot pulled the map out of his reach.

'I can get us there,' he insisted. 'I know just where it is from here.'

Still backing away from Buddie he moved close to Scott who took a first, large, over-eager bite at the eclair. Cream came squirting out of the other end and went all over T-Bob's face.

'What's going on?' he spluttered.

'Er . . . have some eclair, T-Bob,' said the boy, embarrassed.

'Sure is nice of you to share,' replied the robot, scraping the goo off. 'You gave me a real big dollop.'

Buddie chuckled at the incident and teased the boy.

'Scott Trakker – fastest eclair in the west!'

The roar of an engine diverted his attention at once. Buddie looked out through the window in time to see the familiar sight of Jackhammer, an enemy vehicle, as it streaked out of the gateway. It all but knocked down a woman who was wheeling a pushchair. She darted to safety in terror.

Jackhammer vanished in a cloud of dust but not before Buddie had recognised both it and the figure of Cliff Dagger at the driving wheel. The trip to Paris was not going to be a holiday after all. Buddie muttered the one word that spelled disaster. 'VENOM . . .'

THREE

There was a flurry of activity back at the Louvre. The police had been summoned and the place was crawling with detectives and with uniformed gendarmes. Museum officials and security personnel had arrived in force as well, to conduct their own investigations.

But they were all baffled. The Louvre had been broken into and a security officer had been knocked out. Yet nothing was stolen. What was the point of it all? The Frenchmen stood around discussing the crime and gesticulating wildly at each other.

Matt Trakker noticed something that the rest of them missed. When he inspected the paintings which had been turned to face the wall, he saw that they had some strange markings on the back of them. He noted down the markings on a piece of paper so that he could feed the information to his computer later on. Experience told him that he was on to something.

The guide who had shown him around earlier now came up.

'Monsieur Trakker . . .'

'Yes?'

'Telephone call for you. Follow me, please.'

The guide led Matt to a small office and left him alone to take his call. Matt picked up the receiver and spoke into it.

'Hello.'

'It's me,' said Buddie's voice at the other end of the line.

'What gives?'

'You ain't gonna believe this, Matt, but I spotted a VENOM agent.'

'Oh, I believe it, Buddie,' replied Matt with a sigh. 'And it doesn't surprise me. I had a feeling they might be involved in this somehow. Where are you?'

'Right opposite their hideout.'

'What about Scott and T-Bob?'

'They're still with me.'

'I thought you were taking them to the Eiffel Tower.'

'We found a cake shop on the way.'

'That explains it,' said Matt with a chuckle. Then his voice became urgent. 'Right. Give me the directions. Now, what's the name of the street?'

Buddie supplied all the details and Matt noted them down.

'I'd like to try and get inside that house,' added Buddie.

'Good idea.'

'I wanna take a look around.'

'Get Scott and T-Bob away from there first,' ordered Matt. 'We don't want them mixed up in this.'

'Check.'

'I'll get across to you as fast as I can.'

'Terrific.'

'And don't forget, Buddie.'

'Forget what?'

'This is VENOM,' warned Matt. 'Be extra careful.'

'I will.'

Matt Trakker put the receiver down and checked his watch. A minute later, he was leaving the building and climbing into Thunderhawk, his MASK vehicle. Another emergency beckoned.

VENOM had to be stopped yet again.

Buddie Hawkes got back into the cake shop in time to see Scott devour his fourth eclair. T-Bob was cowering behind his map which was now liberally spattered with cream. The proprietress was smiling benignly as she watched from behind the counter.

'Hi, Buddie,' welcomed Scott through a mouthful of eclair. 'Who did you ring from that call box?'

'Your dad.'

'How is he?'

'Fine. He's got a little job for me.'

Scott's ears pricked up at once and he grinned hopefully.

'Is it anything *we* can help with?' he asked.

'Every time you say let's help,' observed T-Bob, 'it's *us* that end up needing the help.'

'T-Bob is right,' agreed Buddie. 'You two have got to stay well clear. Think you can look after yourselves for a bit?'

'Of course!' boasted Scott.

'Let's go find the Eiffel Tower,' said T-Bob.

'With you reading that map,' joked the boy, 'we really *are* going to need help.'

'I'll get you to the Eiffel Tower,' promised the robot. 'It's bound to be more fun than an eyeful of cream!'

Buddie paid the proprietress for all the cakes that had been eaten, then took the others outside. T-Bob took a last peek at his map, then led Scott purposefully off down the road. Buddie waited until they were out of sight before he sprang into action.

He took a closer look at the gateway opposite. The portcullis was not the only security device. Fixed to the wall below it was a black box with a circle of glass set into it.

Buddie recognised it as an electronic eye. It would not prevent him getting into the grounds. He assessed his task and chuckled.

'A piece of cake!'

He went quickly back to Hurricane and took out a large attaché case. Then he ran across the road and down the alley that was close to the wall that surrounded the VENOM hideout.

Buddie paused when he reached a cluster of trashcans. After checking to make sure that he could not be seen, he put the case on a trash-can before opening it. Inside the case was a wide selection of make-up, nose-putty, false hair, moustaches, beards and glasses.

He looked at himself in the mirror fixed inside the lid.

'It's tough, Buddie,' he said to himself. 'I almost can't stand to cover up such a handsome dude – but here goes.'

He selected a jar of make-up and got busy.

Buddie Hawkes was not only the vehicles' specialist in the MASK team, he was also an expert at gathering intelligence. To do this, he often had to infiltrate the underworld. It called for great courage and an ability to change both his voice and appearance.

He needed only a few minutes to effect the change. After putting make-up on his face, he slipped into black trousers and a T-shirt, and then pulled a cap down over one eye. A little padding on the shoulders helped him to thicken out. When he gave a leer, the transformation was complete. He looked ugly, brutal and villainous. An exact replica of Cliff Dagger. Even down to the gruff voice.

Buddie Hawkes was truly a master of disguise.

'Your own mother wouldn't know us apart, Dagger,' he said.

He pulled a bulky handgun from the case and also a thin cable. Hooking them both to his belt, he took a final look at himself in the mirror and heaved a sigh.

'Crying shame, that's what it is. Buddie was so good-looking and now he's plug-ugly.' He shrugged. 'All part of the job, though.'

He closed his case and hid it behind the trash-cans.

Buddie had already decided how he would get inside the VENOM hideout and he now put his plan into action. Standing on a trash-can, he sprang with an athletic leap and caught hold of a window sill on the wall of one of the houses. Slowly but surely, he began to climb upwards by means of toe holds in the old brickwork.

It was a very tricky ascent but, like all MASK agents, he had been well-trained and made light of the problems. Leaning across to grab a drainpipe, he swung himself up on to the roof of the house. He paused to get his breath back and to assess the difficulty of the next stage of his plan.

Buddie was high above the perimeter wall now. The VENOM hideout was only a short distance away from him. His eye ran along the top of the building until he saw an open skylight. That would be his way in.

First of all, he had to reach it.

Uncoiling the cable from his belt, he tied one end of it to the chimney behind him and tested to make sure that it was secure. At the other end of the cable was a long dart. He inserted it into the handgun then aimed it at the nearest chimney on the hideout.

'I just hope Santa Claus isn't in there!' he said.

Pulling the trigger, he sent the cable snaking through the air at high speed. Buddie had to brace himself against the kick of the gun. There was a cloud of white smoke but almost no noise. The metal dart struck the brickwork of the chimney and pierced it at once. When it had gone right through to the other side, the barbs at its head fanned out like an umbrella. The cable was now taut. Buddie Hawkes had his own private means of entry to the hideout.

He took a pulley from his pocket, fixed it to the cable and held on tight with both hands. Pushing himself off the roof, he whizzed along the cable with his body dangling in mid-air.

'Happy landings!' he said to himself.

Then he found himself sitting on the roof of the hideout.

Picking himself up, he ran to the open skylight and climbed through it. He was in an attic that was full of junk and old furniture. He opened the door and crept downstairs.

When he got to the first floor, he opened the door to the room in which Miles Mayhem had been hatching his plot. The place was now empty but the map was still pinned to the wall.

Buddie knew that he had found a vital clue. He crossed to the map and began to study it. What was the significance of the crosses? And why were they joined together by dotted lines?

He gazed up at the map and scratched his head.

The living room at the hideout was as dilapidated as the rest of the house. There was little furniture, no carpet and peeling walls. Chunks of plaster had fallen from the ceiling and the gilt-framed mirror above the mantelpiece was cracked in a thousand places.

Miles Mayhem and Sly Rax were seated at a table playing cards. Stray bills and coins were scattered around. Their masks stood on the floor beside them.

Vanessa Warfield was in the background, adjusting her own mask. She looked across with disdain as the two men started to argue.

'You already played that card,' accused Rax.

'That was last hand,' growled Mayhem.

'No, it wasn't. You just took my Queen with it.'

'You're a liar, Rax!'

'And you're a card-sharper, Mayhem!'

'No, I'm not!'

'Yes, you are!'

Vanessa stepped in before the row got any worse.

'Can't you slobs do anything except cheat each other at penny-ante?' she sneered.

'I wasn't cheating!' denied Mayhem.

'Neither was I!' added Rax.

Vanessa was not impressed with them at all.

'Here we are sitting on millions,' she told them, 'and all you can do is try to squeeze a couple of lousy bucks out of each other.'

'We're just killing the time,' said Mayhem.

'Yeah, that's it,' agreed Rax. 'We're waiting till Dagger gets back with that triggering device.'

'*If* he gets back,' corrected Vanessa. 'Knowing him, he'll probably lose the way.'

'Dagger will get here,' announced Mayhem confidently.

His prediction came true immediately. The door crashed open and a familiar figure burst in.

But which Cliff Dagger was it?

The real one or the fake?

FOUR

Panting from his exertions, the burly figure stood in the middle of the room. Mayhem, Rax and Vanessa stared at him in surprise. He got enough breath back to be able to speak.

'It's me,' he announced. 'Cliff Dagger.'

'We can see that,' said Rax with a snigger.

'Nobody else could look as ugly as you,' observed Vanessa.

Mayhem jumped to his feet and crossed to his henchman.

'Now what?' he demanded. 'I told you to get that thing.'

'I forgot the map,' confessed Dagger.

'Forgot the map?' repeated Mayhem with derision.

'Had a lot on my mind,' claimed Dagger.

'What mind?' snapped Vanessa tartly.

'Dagger!' snapped Mayhem.

'Yeah?'

'You'd forget your own head if it wasn't nailed on.'

'Who'd notice?' said Vanessa, curling her lip.

While Mayhem's back was turned, Rax had been doing his best to sneak a look at the other man's cards. He smiled when he saw that *he* was holding the best hand.

Dagger tried to shrug an apology to his boss.

'Hurry up!' shouted Mayhem. 'You've wasted enough time here.'

'I'm going,' said Dagger.

'Then GO!'

'Okay. I will.'

As soon as Dagger left the room, Mayhem swung around to confront Rax. The latter was doing his best to look innocent. Mayhem went back to the table and snatched up his own cards.

'You looked at my hand!' he accused.

'No, I didn't!' retorted Rax.

'Yes, you did!'

'Prove it!'

'You saw that I got four aces.'

'But you haven't, Mayhem. All you got is two sixes, two sevens and a ten of diamonds.'

Rax gulped as he realised he had given himself away.

Mayhem stood over him and bunched a huge fist.

'If you want to look at my hand – look at this one!'

Buddie Hawkes was still examining the map when the door behind him swung open. He spun round to find himself facing the real Cliff Dagger. Both men were rooted to the spot for a second.

'Hey, it's *me*!' gasped Dagger.

'Yeah, that's right,' said Buddie, imitating his voice.

'What am *I* doing in here already?'

'I'm your twin brother.'

'But I got no twin brother.'

'You have now.'

'Huh?'

While Dagger was still in a state of confusion, Buddie tried to make a getaway. He dived for the nearest window but found that it was locked. Reinforced glass meant that he could not break his way to freedom either. He was trapped.

Dagger let out a roar and lunged at him.

'Come here, you!'

'No, thanks.'

Buddie looked upwards and saw the hanging light directly above him. He jumped up on the window sill so that he could reach the light. Using the chain like a trapeze, the MASK agent pushed himself away from the sill and sailed across the room.

Dagger had to duck right down to avoid being knocked to the floor. Buddie made a soft landing then shot out through the door and slammed it shut behind him.

'Hey, come back here!' yelled his double.

Dagger ran to the door and spent a long time trying to push it open. When he saw that it did, in fact, open inwards, he pulled it towards him so violently that it came off its hinges.

'I'll get him!' he snarled.

Cliff Dagger went charging out after himself.

Downstairs in the living room, the two men had started another game. Vanessa was still attending to her mask and making sarcastic comments about the cardplayers. Both of them were trying to cheat now.

The door opened and Buddie raced across the room.

Mayhem thought it was Dagger and leapt to his feet.

'There you are!'

'Just passing through,' said Buddie, imitating the gruff voice.

'Make it snappy this time!'

'I will.'

'We haven't got all week!' Mayhem blinked in astonishment as the figure shot through the front door. 'Where'd he go?'

'That way!' said Rax, pointing to the door.

As soon as Mayhem looked away, Rax tried to peek at his boss's cards once again. But he had no time. The door to the staircase was flung open once more and Cliff Dagger came lumbering in.

'You just went out!' exclaimed Mayhem.

'No,' insisted Dagger. 'I just come in.'

'Then who was *that*?'

'A spy!'

'Are you sure?'

'He saw the map,' grunted Dagger.

'After him!' ordered Mayhem. 'If even one person catches on to what we're doing, the whole scheme is off!'

The four of them ran to the front door and threw it open. Buddie Hawkes was already halfway down the drive. He was sprinting over the gravel as fast as his legs would carry him.

'He's getting away!' protested Dagger.

'We'll never catch him now,' decided Rax.

'There has to be *some* way to slow him down,' said Vanessa.

'There is,' concluded Mayhem.

The VENOM leader grabbed his Stiletto mask and lowered it on to his head. He stood in the doorway and faced the gatehouse. Then he snapped a command to his mask.

'Stiletto – on!'

There was a loud zapping sound as the mask fired a high-speed dart. It shot through the air, whistled past Buddie's ear then went on to hit the chain that held the portcullis up. The dart had hit its target bang on.

The portcullis began to lower with a clanking sound.

Buddie saw his escape being cut off and tried to accelerate. As he lengthened his stride, however, his foot came up against a large stone and he tripped over

it. Unable to stop himself, he was thrown forward on the gravel and came to a halt beneath the portcullis.

Miles Mayhem was delighted with what he saw.

'Serves him right!' he said with a grim chuckle.

'That oughta cut him down to size,' noted Vanessa.

Buddie Hawkes lay helpless beneath the portcullis. He looked up and saw the iron teeth descending relentlessly towards him. There was no escape this time.

Death seemed certain.

While his agent had been gaining entry to the hideout, Matt Trakker had been finding his way through a maze of streets. He arrived outside the cake shop in the nick of time. As he leapt out of Thunder Hawk, he saw the dart strike the chain and send the portcullis on its murderous journey downwards.

Buddie Hawkes lay sprawled on the ground beneath it.

Matt acted with speed and decision. Diving into Hurricane, he pressed a button on the dashboard. The trunk of the vehicle shot open and the spare tyre was catapulted out.

It reached the portcullis just in time to jam beneath it and save Buddie's life. The spikes were only an inch from his face when they were stopped. Buddie heaved a sigh of relief and dragged himself out from the danger area.

'I guess it's time to re-tyre!' he said.

He scrambled across the road to be greeted by Matt.

'That was a close one, Buddie.'

'Too close for comfort!'

'Just as well some of your make-up had come off,' noted Matt. 'I realised it was you and not Dagger.'

'If it had been him, you'd have let the portcullis fall?'

'You bet your sweet life, Buddie!'

'It was Dagger who caught me inside the house.'

'Was Mayhem there as well?' asked Matt.

'Yeah,' said Buddie. 'So were those other creeps – Sly Rax and Vanessa Warfield.'

'VENOM is here in force, then. Just as I thought.'

Matt Trakker's worst suspicions had been confirmed.

Watching from the front door of the house, Miles Mayhem and his gang had not seen the arrival of Thunder Hawk. All they knew was that a spy had miraculously escaped from beneath the portcullis.

Mayhem drew the only conclusion possible.

'MASK!' he sneered. 'They're on to us.'

'What do we do now?' wondered Dagger.

'Get moving!'

Mayhem led them quickly back into the living room. They picked up their masks and held them under their arms. Mayhem swooped on the card table and swept up his winnings before Rax could stop him.

'Right!' announced the VENOM commander. 'We've got to put our plan into action now or we've lost the whole show!'

'We can't let MASK beat us again!' shouted Vanessa.

'They won't,' vowed Rax.

'What are we waiting for?' urged Dagger.

'Nothing!' said Mayhem. 'Come on!'

They followed him out into a corridor and down the steps that led to the cellar. They came to an underground garage. Parked on the cement floor were three of the distinctive VENOM machines – Manta, Piranha and Jackhammer.

Miles Mayhem pressed a button set into the wall.

There was a loud mechanical whine and a deep crack appeared in the featureless cement. It was a square panel and it swung up to reveal a dark, brickwork tunnel beyond.

Dagger got into Jackhammer and turned on its lights. The powerful beam scoured the tunnel and revealed that there were inches of green water all over its floor. Revving his engine, Dagger moved his vehicle forward then shot off down the tunnel.

The sound of Jackhammer's supercharged engine was magnified inside the hollow brickwork and water sprayed everywhere. Sly Rax went off next in Piranha, his whirring wheels sending up further waves as he plunged off down the tunnel.

Mayhem leapt into Manta beside Vanessa.

'Let's go!' he snapped. 'This could be one of the greatest days that VENOM has ever had. Drive on!'

Vanessa took Manta rocketing off through the murky water.

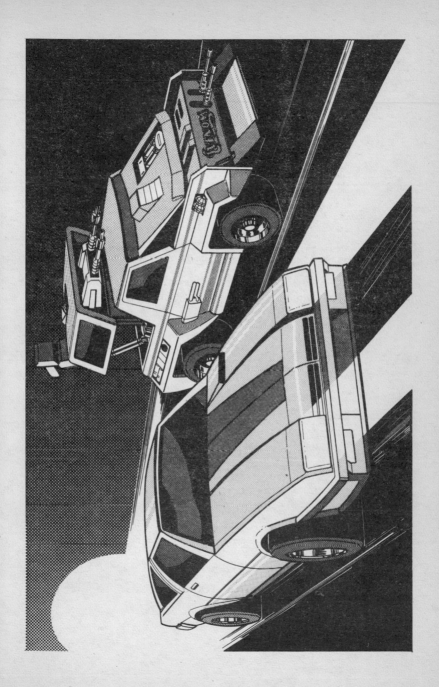

High above them, the city went about its business. Nobody knew the peril that lurked down below. VENOM did not play for small stakes.

The whole of Paris was in danger.

FIVE

Buddie Hawkes reclaimed his attaché case from its hiding place in the alley. He took out a jar of removing cream and began to take off his make-up. The repulsive face of Cliff Dagger soon vanished, to be replaced by the pleasant features of the MASK agent.

He changed back quickly into his own clothes.

'I can't thank you enough, Matt,' he said.

'For what, Buddie?'

'Giving that portcullis something else to bite on.'

'Well, I couldn't let them get the drop on you.'

'Oh!' groaned Buddie. 'That's the worst pun I've ever heard.'

'Sorry. Couldn't resist it.'

They crossed the road and stood beside the MASK vehicles.

'Anyway, I got inside their hideout,' recalled Buddie.

'Yes. Good work!'

'You'll never guess what I found there, Matt.'

'Maybe I will.'

'How?'

'Was it *this*, by any chance?'

Matt reached into Thunder Hawk and pulled out a map of Paris that was identical to the one pinned on the wall in the hideout. Buddy was completely taken aback.

'How did you get that?' he asked.

'The same way that Mayhem did.'

'And how was that?'

'At the Louvre,' explained Matt. 'He did steal something, after all. Some priceless information.'

'I don't understand.'

'You will, Buddie. Hop in your car and follow me. I'll fill you in on the way.'

'Trouble, Matt?'

'Big trouble.'

'We gonna call the team?'

'There's no time for that. It's just you and me.'

'I'm ready,' asserted Buddie. 'Let me get at 'em!'

'That's the spirit,' said Matt. 'By the way, what happened to Scott and T-Bob? Are they safely out of the way?'

'Yeah. They'll be up the Eiffel Tower by now.'

'Fine. Let's hit the road, then!'

'I'm right on your tail!'

Matt jumped into Thunder Hawk and Buddie got behind the driving wheel of Hurricane. The two MASK vehicles powered their way along with a real sense of urgency.

They had to catch VENOM. Fast.

Scott Trakker and T-Bob had seen far more of Paris than they wished to but they could do nothing about it. The robot's directions had taken them everywhere but the Eiffel Tower and both of them were losing faith in the map. They now found themselves in a real quandary.

T-Bob had converted to motorscooter mode and Scott was sitting astride him. They were going round and round the traffic island in the Place de l'Etoile, a notoriously busy part of the city. Hundreds of other vehicles zoomed about and they were unable to reach the safety of the curb. Each time they tried, they were forced to do one more circuit of the traffic island. It was making them both dizzy.

'Holy jumping gear-ratios!' exclaimed T-Bob.

'This is worse than a cattle stampede!' shouted Scott.

'I wanna go back to the Louvre.'

'The Louvre?'

'Yeah. It was so nice and quiet there.'

'T-Bob, we've been round this thing a dozen times so far. How do we get to the Louvre when we can't even get across the street?'

A gap suddenly appeared in the traffic and the robot darted towards it. He veered wildly away as a huge truck lurched into his path. They were bullied into doing yet another circuit.

'This is a real treadmill,' complained the boy.

'It's like a freeway going round in circles.'

'I thought you said you knew the way to the Eiffel Tower.'

'I do!' screamed T-Bob. 'I do!'

'Then take me there.'

'I will when I can get out of this crazy mess!'

T-Bob dodged a car which suddenly cut in front of him then he spurted forward and forced his way across four lanes of traffic. He roused the ire of the Parisian motorists straight away.

Horns were sounded, voices raised and fists waved.

'We're not too popular here,' noted Scott.

A gendarme blew a whistle and tried to stop them.

'If the police are after me, I'm going!' announced T-Bob. 'I didn't come all the way to Paris to see the inside of a cell.'

He accelerated away and threw caution to the winds.

Thunder Hawk and Hurricane, meanwhile, were having their own problems with the city's traffic. But the two vehicles managed to keep up a steady speed without recourse to reckless driving.

As Matt Trakker sat in the first car, the face of Buddie Hawkes came up on the small video screen that was on his dashboard. The voice of the young MASK agent came through on distort.

'Can you hear me, Matt?'

'Loud and clear, Buddie!'

'So what's with the map?'

'I put it together the same way Mayhem did,' he explained. 'Off the backs of those paintings in the Louvre.'

'The *backs*?'

'Yeah. That's why they were turned around.'

'I don't get it.'

'They had top secret information on them.'

'*I* didn't see it, Matt.'

'That's because you didn't know where to look.'

'Huh?'

'The computer will tell you the story.'

Matt pressed a button and his friend's face disappeared from the video screen. In its place came a series of shots of beautiful French paintings. Buddie would be watching them on his own video screen.

The computer spoke in a flat, toneless, female voice.

'These are some of the finest paintings in the Louvre.'

'They sure are!' agreed Matt, seriously.

'During World War II,' continued the computer, 'the French Resistance hid those paintings so that Hitler would not take them.'

A computer-generated map of Paris now came up on the screen with glowing lights indicating various parts of the city.

'Hey!' said Buddie from inside Hurricane. 'That's just like the map back at the hideout. Those lights are in exactly the same spots as the crosses were. What do they represent?'

'Just listen,' suggested Matt, 'and you'll find out.'

'I'm all ears,' promised Buddie.

The computer took up the story once more.

'During the German occupation of Paris, Hitler decided to plant a network of bombs under the city in the sewers. He planned to blow up Paris if the Allies should try to march in.'

The video screen now displayed a computer-generated schematic of a small triggering device. It was a box with an aerial and a switch on it. Even on the screen, it somehow looked highly dangerous.

The computer's voice remained as unemotional as ever.

'The bombs were to be triggered from a distance by this device. A short-wave radio trigger hidden in a sealed bunker.'

'An ancestor of our own remote-control,' noted Matt.

The map of Paris filled the screen again but this time it was superimposed on a plan of the city's sewers. The glowing dots now indicated the locations of the various bombs.

'These are the exact positions of the bombs,' resumed the computer. 'A member of the Resistance found out about them and marked them up on the backs of the paintings that were being kept safe.'

'Why did he do that?' asked Buddie.

'It was probably the only thing they had available to make notes on at the time,' guessed Matt.

'And it was the last place anyone would look,' added the computer. 'The vital information would be stored in a secret place.'

'Hitler never did blow up Paris,' argued Buddie.

'The Germans were forced out too quickly,' said Matt.

'So what happened to the triggering-device?'

'It was never found,' continued the computer. 'After the war, the whole thing was forgotten. Until now.'

'And that's what VENOM is looking for now,' decided Buddie. 'The triggering device.'

'Exactly,' said Matt over the intercom. 'If they find it first, they'll have the whole city in the palms of their dirty hands.'

'So where is that device?'

'The same place that Mayhem used to get into the Louvre.'

'And where's that, Matt?'

'The sewers of Paris!'

Matt Trakker swung Thunder Hawk off the main thoroughfare and drove down towards the river. With Hurricane on his heels, he turned in through a large storm-drain opening and plunged downwards.

MASK was searching in VENOM's natural habitat.

Filthy sewers full of stench and decay.

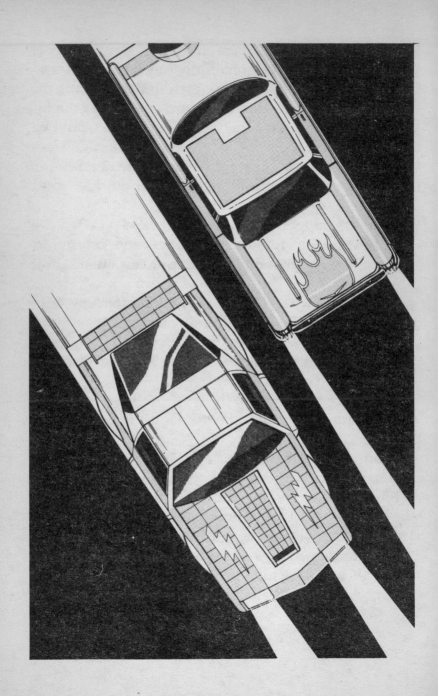

Scott Trakker and T-Bob preferred to look at water above ground. Having failed once more to find the Eiffel Tower, they had come down to the left bank of the River Seine instead. The lovely weather had brought out the artists in their hundreds. Many of them were doing paintings of the mighty Notre-Dame Cathedral but a lot of them seemed to be doing portraits of friends or clients.

T-Bob became quite excited.

'I want them to do me!' he shouted.

'They will if you yell like that,' warned the boy.

'I want to be painted, Scott. Ask one of them.'

'It costs money.'

'They should pay *me*,' argued T-Bob. 'It's not every day that they get a chance to do a portrait of a high-grade robot.'

'Your map-reading hasn't been very high-grade!'

'Let's not talk about that.'

'But I still want to go up the Eiffel Tower.'

'After I've been painted,' said T-Bob. 'I must be painted.'

The robot was so insistent that Scott eventually gave in. He found an artist who was about to go off for a drink in a nearby café. Talking to the man in sign language, the boy managed to get the loan of the artist's brush and palette.

T-Bob was going to be painted in a professional manner.

'Now, stand quite still,' said Scott.

'I will, I will. Oh, it's so thrilling.'

'Ready, T-Bob?'

'Paint away!'

And Scott Trakker did.

Loading his brush with a mixture of colours, he painted a pair of glasses and a big moustache on the robot. Then he added a huge red nose and a set of massive grinning teeth.

T-Bob was not grinning underneath it all.

'Stop it! Stop it at once!' he protested.

'But you told me to paint you!'

Scott was still laughing as he cleaned his robot off.

'*Now* will you take me to the Eiffel Tower?'

'I'll take you anywhere to get away from this paint.'

The robot converted to motorscooter mode and took Scott off at top speed. T-Bob had been caught out red-faced by his artist friend!

The long, low tunnel was made out of mouldering brickwork and several inches of water flowed along it. As Thunder Hawk and Hurricane coasted along, their tyres sent the spray up in great clouds and their headlights created vague, flickering patterns on the circular walls.

Matt Trakker's face was spookily illuminated by the dashboard lights and the glow from the video screen. He drove on bravely through the evil-smelling sewers.

Buddie Hawkes spoke over the intercom.

'It all looks pretty much the same down here.'

'We'll find it, eventually,' assured Matt.

'Where exactly is that triggering device?'

'According to the computer, it's hidden in a sealed bunker. And that bunker is somewhere in this area, Buddie.'

They reached an intersection and slowed down. There was pitch darkness all around. It was very eerie and not a little disturbing. Then the darkness gave way to a dazzling light.

Matt Trakker shielded his eyes from it.

'Ugh!' said Buddie. 'It's VENOM.'

'Prepare for action!' warned Matt. 'They mean business.'

The attack began at once.

SIX

With their guns blazing, two VENOM machines converged on them from opposite directions. Driving Piranha and wearing the Stiletto mask used earlier by Mayhem, Sly Rax came in from the left.

'Not so fast, MASK!' he roared.

Jackhammer raced in from the right with Cliff Dagger behind the driving wheel. He wore his usual Torch mask and spoke with his usual gruff cruelty.

'We'll zap you once and for all, punks!'

The MASK vehicles did not wait for an exchange of greetings. They shot off down the main tunnel and both of them converted to defensive mode. Protective shields came up over the windows and special hoods emerged to enclose their tyres.

Inside Thunder Hawk, the Spectrum mask came down automatically over Matt Trakker's head. Inside Hurricane, the Penetrator mask lowered itself on to the head of Buddie Hawkes. They were now ready for combat against their mortal enemies.

Shells and lasers whistled past them and exploded against the walls of the tunnel. Piranha and Jackhammer were both fitted with a range of weaponry and it was all being deployed as the VENOM agents sought to destroy the vehicles ahead of them.

Buddie spoke to Matt over the intercom.

'This welcome is a bit on the warm side.'

'Where there's rats, you're going to find the cheese.'

'You sound like Bruce Sato,' commented Buddie, referring to another MASK agent. 'He comes up with riddles like that.'

They reached a fork in the tunnel. Thunder Hawk plunged off to the right while Hurricane opted for the left. Their tail-lights were still visible in the darkness as the VENOM machines zoomed up. Piranha went down the tunnel after Thunder Hawk while Jackhammer gave chase to Hurricane.

Matt Trakker had to use all his driving skills to avoid being hit by the laser-fire from his pursuer. He made Thunder Hawk twist and turn and mount the curved walls of the tunnel in order to dodge the lethal bursts of energy that came after him.

Buddie Hawkes, meanwhile, was having difficulty trying to outrun Jackhammer. Shells went past him

every second and they were all perilously close to their target.

'This one is a persistent rat!' muttered Buddie.

He turned down another tunnel and sent more spray against the damp brickwork. When he checked his wing mirrors, however, he had a surprise. The VENOM machine had disappeared. Buddie slowed his own vehicle down and gave a shrug.

'Now where'd he go?'

He got his answer at once.

Jackhammer came at him from the tunnel ahead. Its headlights were blinding and its firepower as fierce as ever. This time, it had an even more deadly weapon.

Cliff Dagger was leaning out of the window so that he could aim his Torch mask at the target. When he was in position, he gave the curt command.

'Torch – on!'

Blazing fireballs shot from his mask and headed straight for Hurricane. Buddie Hawkes took swift evasive action.

'They say sweets for the sweet,' he mused.

Hurricane and Jackhammer were still thundering towards each other. Buddie braked sharply, his vehicle fishtailed and a huge wave of water and mud was thrown up. Leaning out of his machine, Dagger took the full impact and he was plastered. He jammed on the brakes and Jackhammer spun around before squelching to a halt. The fireballs from the Torch mask had fizzled out harmlessly in the water.

'That's a little scum for the scum!' said Buddie.

Dagger was furious. He clutched at the thick, smelly mud and peeled it away from the eyepieces in his mask. When he was able to see again, his fury only increased. The tunnel was quite deserted.

Hurricane had got away.

After another failed attempt to find the Eiffel Tower, Scott Trakker and T-Bob walked alongside the river. The robot consulted his map in the hope that it would actually help him this time.

'The Eiffel Tower's round here some place.'

'That's what you've been saying for the last half-hour,' complained Scott. 'I think your direction finders need overhauling.'

'Well, they certainly don't need *painting* – thank you!'

'Give me that map, T-Bob.'

'I'm the pathfinder,' insisted the robot. 'And I know exactly what direction we're going in.'

'All right, smarty. What direction *are* we going in?'

T-Bob was completely lost and totally flustered.

'Er . . . uh . . . well . . .' He pointed ahead. 'That one!'

Scott walked on a short distance then his eyes rolled in disbelief. He stopped beside what looked like one of the big storm-drains leading out on to the River Seine, except that this one led on to the walkway. The metal grille that usually covered such a drain was missing. There was only a chain across the opening.

Beside the entrance was a large, shapeless object covered in a tarpaulin. It looked quite out of place somehow.

Scott Trakker reacted with genuine enthusiasm.

'Awright!' he announced. 'This must lead into the sewers. We can go and explore!'

'Not on your disc-drive!' protested T-Bob. 'It's *dark* in there.'

The robot stumbled against the solid object and accidentally pulled the tarpaulin away. Something was revealed underneath and it made both of them react with horror.

It was the Switchblade Copter. A VENOM machine.

Miles Mayhem was at the heart of the sewers. He was standing beside the sealed bunker, which was a huge metal wall across one of the tunnels. Manta was parked nearby and Vanessa Warfield leaned against it and watched him. Mayhem was performing a crucial task.

He was wearing his Viper mask and directing it at the metal wall. The corrosive beam from his mask was slowly eating its way into the sealed bunker. Molten metal was dropping on to the floor.

The triggering device would soon be in his hands.

Jackhammer had now joined Piranha in pursuit of Thunder Hawk. Matt was having some trouble in shaking them both off. Laser-fire was zapping all around him, the energy beams making smoking

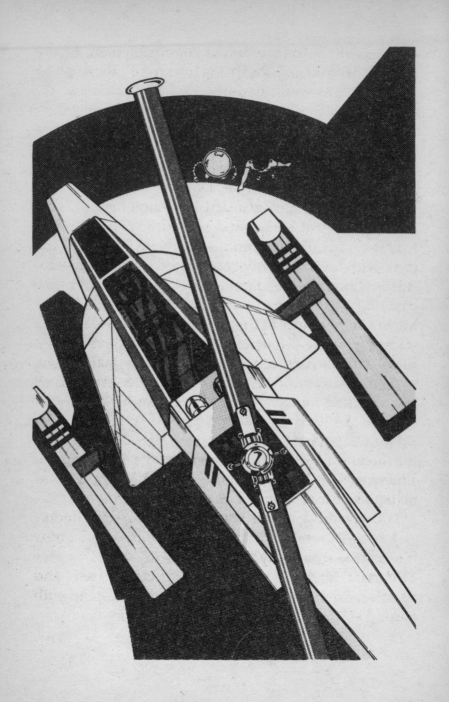

furrows in the brickwork or hissing fiercely in the water. Thunder Hawk's sides were burned by ricochets. The vehicle was weaving desperately up and down the curved walls of the tunnel.

Inexorably, the VENOM machines began to close in.

Sly Rax spoke to his colleague over the intercom.

'We've got him this time, Dagger.'

'Leave him to me!' grunted the other.

But they were both foiled by Buddie Hawkes.

Headlights blinding and lasers blasting, Hurricane came out of a side-tunnel and hared straight at them. Rax was thrown into a panic. He swerved up the side of the tunnel to dodge, and miscalculated how far he could go. He nearly brained himself on the ceiling. Rax slammed on the brakes, swinging Piranha broadside in front of Dagger who brought Jackhammer to another juddering halt and sent up a brown foam all over the walls.

'Where'd they go?' asked Dagger in annoyance.

He could not see them because both Thunder Hawk and Hurricane were driving along with their lights off. The video screens in the respective vehicles were now acting as radar to guide them to safety.

Buddie contacted his leader over the microphone.

'Got you on radar, Matt,' he said. 'Just let me know if you hit a wall, okay?'

Matt Trakker was wearing his Spectrum mask, and its infra-red rays were piercing the gloom ahead with ease.

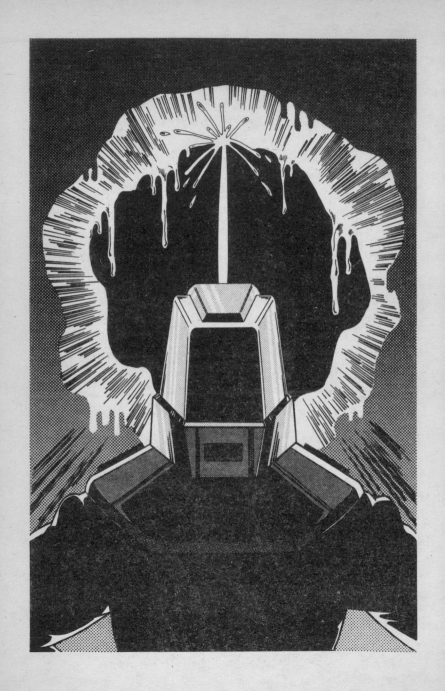

'Don't worry,' he told Buddie. 'I wouldn't leave you in the dark about something like that!'

They shared a laugh and drove on into the blackness.

Miles Mayhem kept at his task until it was completed. A last stream of molten metal poured out and then he stepped back. His mask had now cut a large hole in the solid metal wall. He and Vanessa scrambled through it at once and looked around.

They were in a dingy room with walls of reinforced steel. The only light they had came from the headlights of Manta which was still parked outside. Debris covered the floor. The stink was pungent.

'There it is!' said Vanessa, pointing a bony finger.

'At last!' hissed Mayhem.

They moved towards an old table that stood in the corner. In the middle of it was a bulky steel box with a few knobs and a big red switch on it. At first glance, it looked like a 1940s radio.

Miles Mayhem seized it with glee and lifted it up.

'This is it!' he cackled. 'Now I can destroy the whole of Paris at the flick of a switch.'

He and Vanessa dashed back to their vehicle.

VENOM now had an awesome weapon at their command.

Thunder Hawk and Hurricane were still speeding along in the darkness. The red beam was glowing from

the eyes in Matt's mask. It looked as if two balls of red fire were shooting through the blackness.

A voice was heard over Thunder Hawk's radio.

'Scott calling MASK. Scott calling MASK. Can you hear me?'

Before Matt could answer, his attention was diverted by a threat which had suddenly appeared ahead. Manta was coming straight at them. Its headlights were blazing and its grinding wheels were chomping hungrily, ready to bite a piece out of both MASK vehicles.

Matt and Buddie were equal to the emergency.

As Manta barrelled at them, they swerved up the sides of the tunnel to avoid its crunching grinders. Manta roared between them.

Matt's worst fears were realised.

'They must have the device!' he said over the intercom. 'Don't lose them now, Buddie, or we'll never catch them.'

'Right. Let's go after them.'

Thunder Hawk and Hurricane screeched to a halt then backed into a intersecting tunnel so that they could turn around. Within a split-second, they set off in pursuit.

Scott's voice came over the radio once more.

'Dad? Can you hear me?'

'Yes,' replied Matt. 'Where are you?'

'I've found Switchblade and I'm speaking on its radio,' said the boy, proudly. 'Isn't that clever of me?'

'Very clever, son. But it's also dangerous.'

'Switchblade is parked here by this storm-drain.'

'Never mind that. Just listen to me!'

'Okay.'

'Get out of there right now!'

'Oh, Dad!' protested the boy's voice.

'That's an order, Scott!' insisted Matt, firmly. Go to the Eiffel Tower where you're out of harm's way. Is that clear?'

'Yes, but . . .'

'Do as you're told! Now, go on!'

Matt Trakker concentrated on the job in hand and hurtled down the tunnel after Manta. VENOM simply had to be stopped somehow.

Outside the entrance to the storm-drain, Scott was very disappointed. He had expected praise at least for finding Switchblade and learning to use its radio. Instead of being involved in MASK activities, however, he had been told to stay well clear. It saddened him.

T-Bob, on the other hand, was glad to move on.

'You heard him,' he said. 'Let's go to the Eiffel Tower.'

'How can we when you have no idea where it is?'

'I *do* know,' retorted T-Bob. 'It's on my map.'

'Show me the Eiffel Tower,' challenged the boy.

'Okay, I will.'

The robot grabbed him by the elbow and hurried him up a flight of stone steps. As they came out into the sunlight, they had to shield their eyes from the

glare for a moment. When they looked up, they saw a distinctive shape looming up above them.

It was the Eiffel Tower.

T-Bob was as amazed as Scott but he managed to hide it.

'There you are,' he said airily. 'I told you.'

'Awright!' conceded the boy. 'I guess you don't need a major overhaul, after all.'

'I knew where it was all the time.'

Scott gazed up and his mouth opened in astonishment. The massive structure was even more imposing than he had imagined.

'Boy, it sure is something!' he said.

'Come on,' urged T-Bob. 'Let's go. One thing we do know.'

'What's that?'

'We'll be safe in the Eiffel Tower.'

But T-Bob was wrong.

Instead of leaving danger, they were walking right into it. The Eiffel Tower was a deathtrap for them.

SEVEN

Deep down in the sewers, the chase was as wild and dramatic as ever. Vanessa was coaxing every last ounce of speed from the Manta but the MASK vehicles were still gaining. The pursuit continued through a maze of tunnels. Thunder Hawk and Hurricane got closer and closer.

Then they were confronted by a serious obstacle.

Jackhammer and Piranha came out of a turning ahead of them to form a roadblock. Their guns spat furiously. There was no way through.

Sly Rax sent more laser beams streaking towards them.

'You're not getting past us, MASK!'

'We'll have to go round them,' decided Matt. Then

he spoke over the intercom. 'Buddie – follow me!'

'You got it, Matt.'

Thunder Hawk swerved off down a side-tunnel and out of the range of VENOM guns. Hurricane was on its tail and the two machines were now using their full headlights again.

'I know where Mayhem's coming out,' announced Matt. 'We can still head him off if we hurry.'

But MASK was too late this time.

Even as Matt was speaking, Manta emerged from the storm-drain and stopped to let Mayhem get out. With the triggering device tucked under one arm, he pulled the tarpaulin from Switchblade and got into the machine. He removed his mask and switched on the intercom.

'Dagger, Rax – I'm clear. Keep MASK off till I make our demands.'

Manta now converted to jet mode and picked up speed along the walkway before taking off. Switch-blade converted to helicopter mode and took to the sky in its wake.

It was the moment that Miles Mayhem had dreamed about.

Hitting a button on the dashboard, he grabbed a microphone.

'Attention, people of Paris!'

His voice boomed out across the whole city.

'This is VENOM. There are bombs planted every-where in your sewers. They can destroy the entire city.'

Switchblade was now flying close to the Eiffel Tower. A crowd of tourists peered over the balcony at the top. Among them were Scott Trakker and T-Bob. They heard the next announcement.

'You have one hour to pay me one billion dollars,' warned Mayhem, 'or Paris will be reduced to rubble.'

The tourists on the Eiffel Tower became hysterical.

'You will never find and defuse all the bombs in time,' added Mayhem with a cackle. 'Pay up – or die with your city!'

Panic took over at the top of the Tower. Everyone jumped into the elevators to go back down again. T-Bob was about to join them when he saw that Scott was missing.

'Come on!' yelled the robot. 'We must go down.'

The boy was leaning over the balcony rail.

'Look at that,' he said, pointing down.

Switchblade was now rising from the bank of the Seine and getting closer still to the Eiffel Tower. Thunder Hawk emerged in a flash of speed from the storm-drain and converted to jet mode. Its door flew outwards to form gull-like wings and it rose to the sky.

Manta immediately swooped down on Thunder Hawk and opened fire with its laser-guns. A fierce aerial battle was now under way. Thunder Hawk was pursuing Switchblade and trying to shoot the helicopter down while it was itself the quarry of Manta. Shots and explosions echoed across the sky and thousands of people looked up and watched.

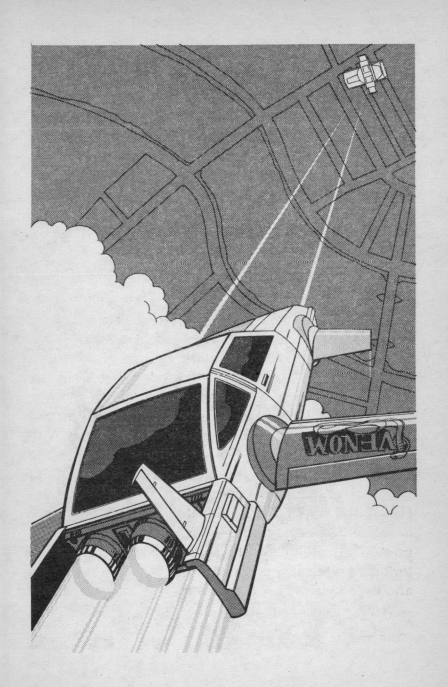

Scott and T-Bob were now the only two left at the top of the Eiffel Tower. The boy was delighted with his grandstand view.

'Hey! Isn't it great up here?'

'No,' said T-Bob, shaking all over.

He soon had even more cause to shake. Manta unleashed another burst of fire at Thunder Hawk. A stray blast nicked one of the iron legs supporting the Tower and it buckled slightly.

The balcony at the top tilted violently. Scott and T-Bob were thrown against the railings and grabbed them just in time. They were lucky not to be hurled out into space.

Screams were heard down below in the street. T-Bob was too hoarse to scream. His voice was querulous and piping.

'Get me down from here!' he pleaded.

The Tower sagged even more, shaking the balcony again.

'I didn't mean that way!' protested the robot.

They clung on desperately and watched the battle continue.

Buddie Hawkes had now joined in. Parking Hurricane at the foot of the Tower, he had converted to attack mode and was firing at Manta with anti-aircraft guns. When he saw the damage done to the leg that supported the Tower, he provided an instant repair. Aiming his guns at the broken area, he bathed the metal in laser beams until the pieces were welded back together again.

The Eiffel Tower was now marginally safer.

Buddie was soon busy firing his guns again. Jackhammer and Piranha came towards him and circled around him as they peppered him with lasers. Like a cowboy holding off an Indian attack from inside a circle of wagons, Buddie fired back and kept the VENOM agents at bay.

High above him, Matt Trakker was in difficulty.

Switchblade converted in mid-air to jet mode and fired a stinger missile straight at Thunder Hawk. It clipped the tail of the MASK aircraft and sent it into a spin.

'You won't catch me this time, Trakker!' boasted Mayhem.

Matt struggled with the controls and spoke over the intercom.

'Buddie, I can't hold them much longer.'

Manta dived in at him again and tried to strafe him. Though he did all he could, Matt could not prevent Thunder Hawk from spiralling downwards. Smoke began to spout from his engines.

'If they get away,' he said over the intercom, 'we'll never catch them in time to stop them blowing up the city.'

Mayhem's face was now radiating an unholy delight.

'Now I'll ground you for good!' he threatened.

Thunder Hawk fell through the air and Scott gasped in horror.

'Dad!' he called.

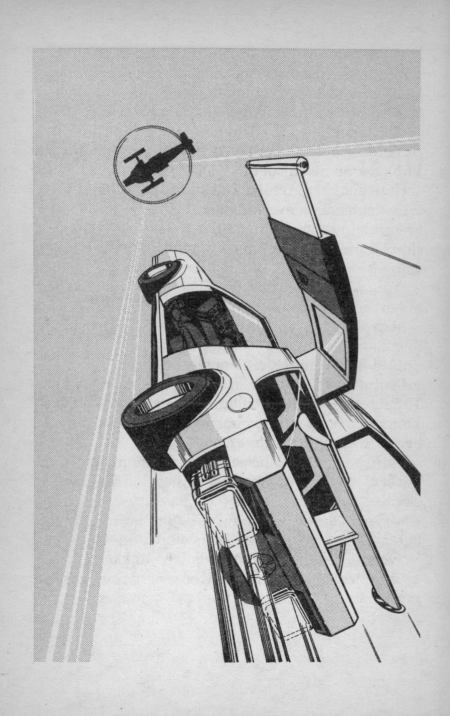

As it continued to spiral downwards, the smoke from its engines became a black pall. Switchblade went into a dive to follow it and destroy it when it reached the ground. Mayhem was bent on eliminating MASK altogether. As Thunder Hawk finally landed, Mayhem opened fire. His lasers bit into the ground and sent up clouds of dust. They also had the advantage of making Piranha and Jackhammer veer away from their attack on Hurricane.

Buddie was given some freedom at last. He made good use of it. Pulling on his Penetrator mask, he leapt into Thunder Hawk beside Matt. The aircraft roared skywards again and aimed straight for Switchblade.

Mayhem reacted with fear and confusion.

Matt Trakker signalled the correct moment.

'Now!' he ordered.

'Penetrator mask!' called Buddie. 'On!'

Thunder Hawk was bathed in the ray from the Penetrator mask just as it reached Switchblade. Its molecular structure was altered and it passed straight through the other jet.

As it did so, Buddie grabbed the box from Mayhem's hands.

'Hey!' shouted the VENOM boss. 'The triggering device is gone.'

'That's because we have it!' said Buddie.

'Paris is safe,' added Matt.

Thunder Hawk was now visible again. Manta moved in for the kill but the MASK aircraft was too quick for it. Swinging around, it fired a flash-bomb at

Manta. It caused the VENOM jet to veer madly around the sky with its guns still blazing. One of its stray shots clipped the nose off a gun mounted on Switchblade.

Miles Mayhem had had enough. He spoke over the radio.

'Come on, Vanessa. We're getting out of here!'

The two aircraft retreated at top speed.

Down below in the street, Jackhammer and Piranha turned tail as well. They knew when they were beaten.

Thunder Hawk was about to pursue the enemy aircraft when there was a loud, creaking noise from the Eiffel Tower. It sagged even more and Scott was left dangling from the balcony with T-Bob. Even in that perilous position, the boy's first thought was of defeating VENOM.

'Go after them, MASK! Don't let them get away!'

'No, no,' begged T-Bob. 'Come back. *Let* them get away.'

Matt Trakker took one look at the Tower.

'We'll take care of VENOM later,' he decided.

'What are you going to do?' asked Buddie.

'Take Thunder Hawk down,' instructed the other. 'I've got some flying of my own to do.'

Matt adjusted his Spectrum mask and snapped an order.

'Spectrum hang-glide – on!'

The mask converted to free-fall facility and he was able to fly across the sky towards the Eiffel Tower. Just when they could hang on no longer, Scott and T-Bob saw Matt descending towards them. He grasped them with an arm each and then flew gently down to the ground.

T-Bob was trembling like a leaf but Scott had loved it.

'You shoulda gone after them, Dad. We'd 've been okay.'

Matt looked upwards and gave a grim smile.

'Knowing VENOM, I'm sure we'll have another chance.'

All four of them went out for a meal that evening in a sidewalk café. Matt and Buddie were in civilian clothes again. Scott studied the menu for eclairs and T-Bob was poring over his precious map.

'So that's it,' said Matt. 'The bombs have all been found and defused, the Eiffel Tower has been repaired, and the triggering device is just another curiosity in the Paris war museum.' He turned to Scott. 'We still have a coupla days left in Paris. Is there anything you still want to see?'

'I'd kind of like to see the Casbah!' admitted T-Bob.

'The Casbah?' repeated Matt. 'Let me see that map of yours, T-Bob.' As soon as Matt studied it, he realised why they had had so much trouble finding their way around. 'This is not a map of Paris. What you've got here is a map of Algiers!'

All four of them enjoyed a long, happy laugh.

Get ready for . . .

MASK 3 – VENICE MENACE
VENOM leader Miles Mayhem's evil scheme to dominate the world, has brought Venice – the city of canals – to a mysterious halt. But MASK is close at hand.

MASK 4 – BOOK OF POWER
The revered Book of Power, holder of mystical and ancient secrets, is sought by VENOM's cunning leader, whose wicked intention is to turn its magic to his own ends. MASK has another urgent mission to follow.

MASK 5 – PANDA POWER
When all the Chinese pandas are stolen from the nature preserves, MASK is not long in finding out who lies behind the crime. Why a celebrated sculptor should be kidnapped as well though, is more puzzling, and increases the alarm.

KNIGHT BOOKS

Five stunning MASK adventures from Knight Books

☐	39890 6	MASK 1 – The Deathstone	£1.95
☐	39891 4	MASK 2 – Peril Under Paris	£1.95
☐	39892 2	MASK 3 – Venice Menace	£1.95
☐	39977 5	MASK 4 – Book of Power	£1.95
☐	40327 6	MASK 5 – Panda Power	£1.95

All these books are available at your local bookshop or newsagent, or can be ordered direct from the publisher. Just tick the titles you want and fill in the form below.

Prices and availability subject to change without notice.

Knight Books, P.O. Box 11, Falmouth TR10 9EN, Cornwall.

Please send cheque or postal order, and allow the following for postage and packing:

U.K. – 55p for one book, plus 22p for the second book, and 14p for each additional book ordered up to a £1.75 maximum.

B.F.P.O. and EIRE – 55p for the first book, plus 22p for the second book, and 14p per copy for the next 7 books, 8p per book thereafter.

OTHER OVERSEAS CUSTOMERS – £1.00 for the first book, plus 25p per copy for each additional book.

Please send cheque or postal order (no currency).

Name ....

Address ....

....